In The Shadow of Shani Dev Ji

Mrigendra Bharti

Published by Sellbrochure Vymish Entertainment, 2024.

IN THE SHADOW OF SHANI DEV JI

First edition. July 7, 2024.

Copyright © 2024 Mrigendra Bharti.

ISBN: 979-8227545411

Written by Mrigendra Bharti.

Table of Contents

Preface

In the realm of Hindu mythology, Shani Dev, the Lord of Saturn, stands as a formidable figure, his influence extending far beyond the celestial realm. His gaze, piercing and unforgiving, is said to hold the power to mete out justice, karmic retribution for the deeds of mortals. And yet, amidst this aura of sternness, there lies a profound wisdom, a recognition of the inescapable consequences of our actions.

"In The Shadow of Shani Dev Ji" weaves a tale that interlaces the cosmic tapestry with the intricate threads of human existence. We follow the journey of an individual whose life has been indelibly marked by the influence of Shani Dev. As this individual navigates the challenges and triumphs that life presents, they find themselves grappling with the weight of karmic burdens and the inescapable gaze of Shani Dev.

This story is not merely a narrative of fate and destiny; it is a profound exploration of the human condition, a testament to the resilience of the spirit in the face of adversity. We witness the protagonist's struggles with self-doubt, the temptation to succumb to despair, and the unwavering belief in the possibility of redemption.

Amidst the trials and tribulations, the protagonist discovers the transformative power of self-awareness and the unwavering pursuit of righteousness. They learn to embrace the lessons imparted by Shani Dev, recognizing that even in the darkest of times, there lies the potential for growth and enlightenment.

"In The Shadow of Shani Dev Ji" is a story that transcends the boundaries of culture and belief. It speaks to the universal human experience of facing our karmic debts, striving for redemption, and ultimately, finding liberation from the shackles of our past. It is a tale that will linger in your mind long after the final page is turned, prompting introspection and inspiring self-reflection.

Prologue

In the churning expanse of the cosmos, where stars shimmered like celestial dust and celestial beings danced to the rhythm of time, resided Shani Dev, the embodiment of karma. His gaze, a piercing indigo, surveyed the mortal realm, a vast tapestry woven with the threads of countless lives. Each action, each decision, from the grandest act of heroism to the most fleeting thought, left an indelible mark, a ripple in the fabric of existence.

For eons untold, Shani Dev had maintained the balance, ensuring that every deed found its consequence, both the virtuous and the vile. Yet, a disharmony stirred within the mortal realm. The whispers of injustice grew louder, shrouding the land in a shadow of corruption and despair. The scales of karma teetered on the precipice, threatening the delicate equilibrium upon which all creation rested.

It was amidst this growing imbalance that an extraordinary event unfolded. A celestial alignment, a convergence of planets unseen for millennia, cast an otherworldly glow upon the mortal realm. This convergence, whispered of in ancient prophecies, heralded a time of reckoning, a pivotal moment where the course of karma could be altered.

Acknowledgment

Dear Reader,

As I complete this book, I offer my heartfelt gratitude for your invaluable support and inspiration.

As a writer, I understand that any creative work may contain imperfections. If this book contains any inaccurate facts, misinterpretations, or any offensive material, I sincerely apologize. My intention was never to cause offense or disrespect to anyone.

Throughout this creative journey, I have drawn inspiration and guidance from Shani Dev Ji. If any errors or mistakes in this book stem from my ignorance or oversight, I humbly seek forgiveness from Shani Dev Ji.

YOUR FEEDBACK AND SUGGESTIONS are incredibly valuable to me. If this book has inspired you or provided a learning opportunity, I consider that a great privilege.

With best wishes,

Mrigendra Bharti

About Sellbrochure Vymish Entertainment

Sellbrochure Vymish Entertainment, recognized as India's largest book publishing company, has made significant strides in ensuring its extensive collection of books reaches audiences across the global market. This rapid expansion is a testament to the company's dedication to disseminating knowledge and literature far beyond national borders. Central to its success is its affiliation with InkWhirl Media Networks, a reputable entity in the media and publication industry known for its innovative and strategic approaches. Within this network, InkWhirl Publication LLC operates as a vital division, further enhancing the company's capabilities and reach in the international market.

The visionary behind this enterprise is Mrigendra Bharti, the founder of Sellbrochure Vymish Entertainment. His foresight and passion for the literary world have been instrumental in steering the company towards remarkable growth and recognition. Under his leadership, Sellbrochure Vymish Entertainment has not only expanded its catalog but also established a strong presence in both domestic and international markets. Mrigendra Bharti's commitment to excellence and innovation has been a driving force in the company's journey, ensuring that it stays ahead of industry trends and meets the evolving needs of readers worldwide.

Sellbrochure Vymish Entertainment operates under the robust support of its parental organization, Mrigendra Bharti Group InfoTech. This affiliation provides the necessary resources and strategic guidance, enabling the publishing company to undertake ambitious projects and explore new markets. Mrigendra Bharti Group InfoTech's extensive experience in technology and information services has been a valuable asset, allowing Sellbrochure Vymish Entertainment to integrate advanced digital solutions in its operations, thereby enhancing its distribution capabilities and reader engagement.

Through relentless efforts and a commitment to quality, Sellbrochure Vymish Entertainment continues to break barriers and expand the reach of Indian literature globally. The company's diverse portfolio includes a wide range of genres, catering to different age groups and interests, thereby fostering a rich and inclusive reading culture. As it continues to innovate and grow, Sellbrochure Vymish Entertainment remains dedicated to its mission of making literature accessible to all, contributing significantly to the global literary landscape.

Connect With Mrigendra,
Thank you very much for choosing this book.
You can also connect with me on Instagram,
https://www.instagram.com/i_mrigendrabharti.official
With Love,
Mrigendra Bharti

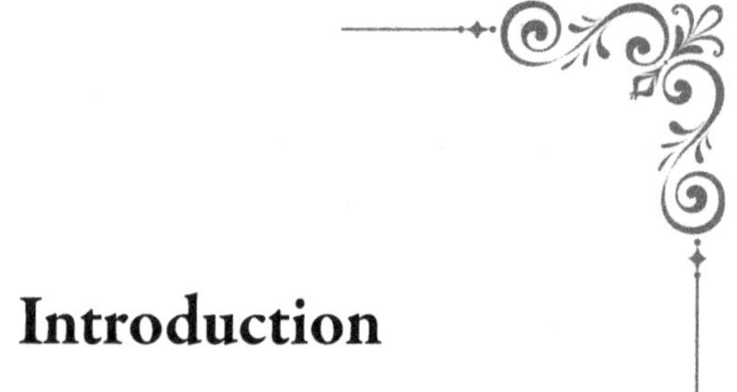

Introduction

Welcome, dear reader, to a realm where the whispers of the cosmos intertwine with the destinies of mortals. Here, in the shadow of Shani Dev, the Lord of Karma, unfolds a tale that transcends the boundaries of time and space. It is a story etched in the celestial tapestry, its threads woven with the triumphs and tribulations of those entangled in the inescapable web of karmic consequences.

This is not merely a chronicle of events, but an invitation to embark on a profound journey of self-discovery. As you delve deeper into the narrative, prepare to confront the universal human struggles – the allure of power, the sting of betrayal, the yearning for redemption. Through the experiences of our characters, you will witness the transformative power of karma, a force that not only dictates consequences but also offers opportunities for growth and enlightenment.

Within these pages, you will encounter a world where celestial beings observe the mortal drama, their interventions tipping the scales of fate. You will meet individuals whose lives are irrevocably marked by Shani Dev's gaze, forced to confront the repercussions of their choices. Yet, amidst the shadows, glimmers of hope emerge. Acts of compassion, courageous decisions, and unwavering faith in justice illuminate the path towards a more balanced existence.

Whether you are a seasoned explorer of mythology or a curious seeker of wisdom, "In The Shadow of Shani Dev Ji" promises a captivating adventure. Prepare to be enthralled by the intricacies of karma, challenged by the complexities of human nature, and ultimately, inspired by the enduring power of the human spirit to rise above adversity. So, turn the page, dear reader, and step into a world where every action echoes through eternity, shaping not only individual destinies but the very fate of the cosmos itself.

Chapter 1: An Unusual Birth

In the celestial expanse, where constellations shimmered like scattered diamonds, lay Surya Loka, the resplendent abode of Surya Dev, the Sun God. Its majestic gates, carved from sunstone, shimmered with an otherworldly luminescence. Inside, celestial artisans crafted intricate tapestries depicting the sun's glorious journey across the heavens. The very air vibrated with a radiant energy, a testament to Surya Dev's divine presence.

Surya Dev, seated upon a throne sculpted from a celestial pearl, exuded an aura of unparalleled brilliance. His skin, the color of burnished gold, emanated warmth that banished even the faintest celestial chill. His eyes, like molten spheres of fire, held the power to illuminate the darkest corners of the cosmos. He was the embodiment of righteousness, his gaze unwavering as he ensured the day unfolded according to the cosmic order.

Chhaya Rani, Surya Dev's consort, was a vision of serenity in her abode adjacent to the grand court. Her laughter, like the tinkling of wind chimes, brought a sense of calm to the vibrancy of Surya Loka. Her sapphire-hued skin, the color of a twilight sky, held a depth that mirrored the vastness of space. Her eyes, pools of liquid moonlight, shone with a gentle luminescence that soothed even the most troubled souls. Chhaya Rani was the embodiment of compassion, her presence a balm to the intensity of Surya Dev's radiance.

Their union was a harmonious dance between celestial fire and ethereal grace. Together, they ensured the delicate balance between day and night, light and shadow, warmth and tranquility. It was a union that nurtured life across the cosmos, a testament to the interconnectedness of seemingly opposing forces.

For countless eons, their life flowed in a rhythm as ancient as time itself. Surya Dev faithfully performed his celestial duties, his chariot illuminating the heavens with unwavering dedication. Chhaya Rani maintained an atmosphere of serenity within their abode, her gentle presence a constant source of solace.

One day, a tremor of anticipation rippled through Surya Loka. Chhaya Rani, her divine form radiating an otherworldly luminescence, carried within her the promise of a new life. A palpable excitement filled the celestial court. The arrival of a child into the union of Surya Dev and Chhaya Rani was an event of immense significance, a potential herald of a new era.

The news reached all corners of the cosmos, and celestial beings of every stature gathered in Surya Loka to witness the momentous occasion. The air thrummed with anticipation as the day of the birth arrived.

The celestial court of Surya Loka pulsed with an expectant hush. Chhaya Rani, cloaked in an ethereal glow, emanated an aura of strength and serenity. Surya Dev, his brilliance dimmed with a flicker of apprehension, paced restlessly beside her. The arrival of their child was a moment long awaited, yet an inexplicable disquiet gnawed at Surya Dev's heart.

As the celestial midwives, divine beings renowned for their wisdom and skill, ushered in the birth, an unnatural stillness descended upon the court. The brilliance that usually accompanied the arrival of a celestial child was absent. Instead, an eerie luminescence, tinged with an inky blackness, filled the birthing chamber.

A gasp of collective shock rippled through the court as Chhaya Rani gave birth. The child, unlike any witnessed before, emerged with skin as dark as the void between stars. His eyes, devoid of the usual celestial luminescence, shone with an intense, unsettling glint. An inky mark, shaped like a crow, adorned his forehead, a stark contrast to the usual radiant birthmarks of celestial beings.

A wave of stunned silence washed over the court. The celestial midwives, their faces etched with concern, exchanged worried glances. This was no ordinary child. An unsettling aura, a strange mixture of immense power and a hint of something ominous, emanated from the infant.

Surya Dev, his face etched with a mixture of awe and trepidation, approached the cradle cautiously. He reached out a hesitant hand, the celestial light that usually cloaked him flickering momentarily. As his hand neared the child, a wave of intense heat surged forth, pushing him back. The infant, his dark eyes fixated on Surya Dev, let out a cry that echoed with an otherworldly power, a sound that sent shivers down the spines of even the most seasoned celestial beings.

A cold dread crept into Surya Dev's heart. An inexplicable fear, unlike anything he had ever experienced, washed over him. This child, born under such unusual circumstances, radiated an aura of immense power, yet it was a power laced with an unsettling darkness.

Murmurs of unease rippled through the stunned celestial court. The birth of Surya Dev and Chhaya Rani's child, shrouded in such extraordinary circumstances, had shaken their sense of cosmic order. The unsettling darkness that clung to the infant, the intensity of his gaze, and the unexplainable rejection by Surya Dev himself fueled whispers of an ominous prophecy.

Legends spoke of a celestial being, born under a dark star, who would bring chaos and disruption to the cosmos. The child's unusual appearance and the unsettling aura he exuded sparked fears of this prophecy coming to pass.

Whispers turned to hushed discussions among the celestial beings. Advisors with furrowed brows exchanged worried glances. Even the usually stoic guards, their expressions grim, gripped their celestial weapons a little tighter. The joyous anticipation that had filled the court had been replaced by a pervasive sense of unease.

Chhaya Rani, her heart heavy with a mother's love, remained undeterred by the disquiet surrounding her child. Cradling him close, she showered him with her gentle touch and soothing words. Her unwavering love formed a protective cocoon around the infant, a beacon of serenity amidst the growing storm of anxieties.

Surya Dev, his celestial brilliance dimmed with worry, wrestled with his emotions. The immense power emanating from his child was undeniable, yet it was a power that felt alien, unsettling. The memory of the child's fiery rejection still sent shivers down his spine. He yearned to embrace his son, to fulfill his paternal duties, yet an inexplicable fear held him back.

Torn between his apprehension and his celestial duty, Surya Dev sought counsel from the most wise and revered beings in the cosmos. He consulted with Brahma Dev, the creator, and Vishnu Dev, the preserver. They listened intently to his concerns, their expressions grave. The birth of his son, they acknowledged, was an anomaly, a celestial event shrouded in mystery.

They advised Surya Dev to commission a birth chart, a celestial map depicting the alignment of the stars at the time of the child's birth. This chart, they explained, might hold the key to unraveling the mystery surrounding the child, his unique abilities, and his potential role in the cosmic order.

With a heavy heart, Surya Dev commissioned the creation of a celestial birth chart. He entrusted this vital task to Kashyapa, the great architect of the cosmos, renowned for his knowledge of the stars and their celestial alignments. Kashyapa, his brow furrowed in concentration, meticulously charted the positions of the constellations at the precise moment of the child's birth.

Days turned into weeks as Kashyapa pored over the intricate celestial map. The air crackled with tension as Surya Dev and Chhaya Rani awaited his verdict. Finally, Kashyapa emerged from his celestial observatory, his expression a solemn mix of awe and apprehension.

He summoned Surya Dev and Chhaya Rani to his sanctum, a chamber adorned with celestial charts and shimmering star maps. Kashyapa unveiled the birth chart, its intricate patterns glowing with an otherworldly luminescence. As they gazed upon the chart, a collective gasp escaped their lips.

The celestial alignments spoke of a destiny unlike any other. The child, born under the conjunction of a malevolent star and a powerful celestial body, possessed immense potential. He was destined to be a force of immense justice, a balancer of karma, wielding the power to dispense both fortune and misfortune with an unwavering hand.

The birth chart revealed that the child's dark appearance and unsettling gaze were not signs of evil, as some had feared. They were manifestations of his unique celestial nature, a mark of the immense power and responsibility that lay upon his shoulders.

Kashyapa explained that the child's destiny was intertwined with the very fabric of the cosmos. He would be the overseer of karma, ensuring that every action had an equal reaction, that justice was served, and that the cosmic order remained in balance.

A wave of emotions washed over Surya Dev and Chhaya Rani. Relief mingled with apprehension as they grappled with the implications of Kashyapa's revelation. Their son was not a harbinger of chaos, but a vital cog in the celestial machinery. Yet, the immense power he possessed and the weight of his destiny filled them with a sense of trepidation.

Chhaya Rani, her heart brimming with maternal love, vowed to stand by her son, to guide him through his extraordinary journey. Surya Dev, his apprehension gradually replaced by a sense of acceptance, acknowledged his paternal duty. He would ensure his son received the training and guidance he needed to fulfill his celestial purpose.

The birth of their son, shrouded in mystery and marked by unease, had taken an unexpected turn. The celestial chart had revealed a destiny far grander than anyone could have imagined. The child, yet unnamed, was poised to play a pivotal role in the cosmos, forever etching his mark on the celestial tapestry.

Chapter 2: Early Life and Celestial Whispers

Years flowed by in Surya Loka, each marked by the extraordinary growth of Surya Dev and Chhaya Rani's son. They named him Shani, and his very name carried the weight of his celestial destiny – the dispenser of justice, the upholder of karma.

Unlike other celestial children who basked in the warmth and light of Surya Loka, Shani thrived in solitude. He gravitated towards the serene tranquility of the celestial gardens, often found amidst the shade of ancient banyan trees, their gnarled roots like the claws of time. Here, amidst the whispering leaves and the gentle hum of celestial bees, Shani would contemplate the vastness of the cosmos, his dark eyes reflecting an ancient wisdom beyond his years.

Chhaya Rani, ever the embodiment of nurturing love, showered Shani with her unwavering affection. She understood the weight of his destiny and the isolation it imposed. Her gentle guidance and soothing presence served as a constant source of solace for Shani, a reminder of the love that resided beyond the celestial obligations that awaited him.

Surya Dev, his initial apprehension replaced by a quiet respect for his son's unique nature, observed Shani from afar. The immense power that crackled around Shani demanded a respect that transcended their father-son bond. Surya Dev knew the vital role Shani was destined to play, and he ensured Shani received the training necessary to wield his power with wisdom and justice.

One day, as Shani wandered through the celestial gardens, lost in contemplation, a booming voice echoed through the air. Startled, he looked up to see a majestic figure materialize before him. It was Brahma Dev, the creator, his four heads adorned with celestial crowns, his presence radiating an aura of immense wisdom and power.

Brahma Dev regarded Shani with a penetrating gaze that seemed to pierce through the very fabric of his being. "Shani," he boomed, his voice resonating like thunder, "you are a being of immense potential, destined to play a crucial role in the grand cosmic dance."

Shani, ever respectful, bowed his head in deference. "Esteemed Brahma Dev," he replied, his voice a low rumble, "I am but a child, unsure of the path that lies before me."

A gentle smile touched Brahma Dev's lips. "Your path, Shani, is already ordained. You are the embodiment of karma, the upholder of justice. Yours is the responsibility to ensure that every action has an equal reaction, that the scales of cosmic balance are never tipped."

Shani listened intently as Brahma Dev expounded upon his celestial duty. The weight of his destiny, though daunting, filled him with a sense of purpose. He understood that his power was not meant for destruction, but for maintaining the delicate equilibrium of the cosmos.

"Justice, Shani," Brahma Dev continued, "is not about punishment, but about restoring balance. Your gaze, imbued with the power of karma, will reflect the true nature of an individual's deeds. The righteous will have nothing to fear, while those who sow discord will reap the consequences of their actions."

Shani's dark eyes flickered with a faint luminescence, a hint of the immense power he possessed. He yearned to understand this power, to learn how to wield it with fairness and wisdom.

"Your training, Shani," Brahma Dev said, his voice softening, "will be overseen by the wisest gurus in the celestial realm. They will hone your abilities, teach you the intricacies of karma, and instill in you the virtues of impartiality and compassion."

With a wave of his hand, Brahma Dev summoned a celestial chariot, its form shimmering with stardust. "Come, Shani," he boomed gently. "Your journey begins now."

Shani cast a final glance at the serene gardens, a place that had offered him solace and contemplation. He knew his time here was over. With a nod to his mother, who stood watching from afar, a silent tear glistening on her cheek, Shani boarded the chariot.

As the chariot soared through the celestial expanse, Shani stole a glance at Brahma Dev. The creator god's gaze held a hint of sadness, a flicker of empathy for the burden Shani was destined to carry.

Their journey took them to distant corners of the cosmos, where Shani honed his celestial abilities under the tutelage of revered gurus. There was Brihaspati, the wise counselor, who imparted the knowledge of the cosmos and the intricate workings of karma. There was Shukracharya, the teacher of demons, who offered a contrasting perspective, teaching Shhani the art of discernment and the importance of understanding the root causes of actions.

Years turned into eons as Shani immersed himself in his training. He learned to discern the true nature of beings, to see beyond the facade and into the very core of their existence. He practiced wielding his gaze, ensuring it reflected the perfect balance of justice and mercy.

Through his training, Shani developed an air of quiet stoicism. The weight of his destiny etched a seriousness upon his young face. Yet, beneath the stoic exterior, a spark of compassion remained, a flicker of his mother's nurturing love.

As eons bled into one another, Shani's celestial training neared its completion. His mastery over his power was undeniable. His gaze, once a source of unease, now held a profound wisdom, reflecting the true essence of karma. The celestial gurus marveled at his progress, recognizing the immense potential that resided within him.

One day, as Shani meditated beneath a celestial banyan tree, its branches laden with stars like shimmering fruit, a blinding light engulfed him. He opened his eyes to find himself bathed in the radiant glow of Brahma Dev, who had materialized before him.

"Shani," boomed Brahma Dev's voice, "your training is complete. You have mastered your abilities and possess the wisdom to wield them with justice and discernment."

Shani bowed his head in reverence. "Esteemed Brahma Dev," he replied, his voice a low rumble, "I am grateful for the knowledge and guidance you have bestowed upon me."

Brahma Dev smiled gently. "You have earned this knowledge, Shani. Now, it is time for you to assume your celestial duty."

With a wave of his hand, Brahma Dev conjured a magnificent chariot, its form crafted from celestial jade and drawn by crows with wings that shimmered like obsidian. This chariot, Brahma Dev explained, would be Shani's constant companion, a symbol of his unique position as the upholder of karma.

Shani, his gaze lingering on the obsidian crows, felt a strange sense of kinship with these creatures often associated with ill omens. He understood that true justice, like a crow, did not shy away from the shadows, but rather sought truth wherever it may lie.

Brahma Dev then bestowed upon Shani a final and most significant gift – a boon. "Shani," he proclaimed, "whomever you gaze upon shall be reminded of their karmic debts. Your gaze will be a catalyst for introspection and a reminder to rectify past wrongs."

Shani received this boon with a heavy heart. He understood its power and the potential consequences. The ability to confront beings with their karmic burdens was a formidable responsibility, one that could bring both enlightenment and hardship.

"Remember, Shani," Brahma Dev continued, his voice grave, "justice is not always swift or pleasant. It is a process of restoration, a journey of self-realization. Wield your power with wisdom and compassion, for true justice is tempered with mercy."

Shani bowed his head deeply. The weight of his destiny pressed down upon him, yet he was resolute. He would fulfill his celestial duty, ensuring the cosmic scales remained balanced and that justice, however harsh, prevailed.

With a final nod to Brahma Dev, Shani ascended his celestial chariot. The obsidian crows cawed a haunting melody as they launched into the celestial expanse. Shani, his heart filled with a mix of trepidation and determination, steered the chariot towards Surya Loka, the place where his celestial journey began.

News of Shani's impending arrival had spread like wildfire through the celestial court. A wave of hushed anticipation rippled through the once-uneasy court. Surya Dev and Chhaya Rani awaited their son's return, their hearts brimming with a complex mix of emotions – pride in his accomplishments, apprehension for his burden, and a longing for the carefree child who once wandered the celestial gardens.

As Shani's chariot emerged from the celestial void, a hush fell over the court. All eyes turned towards the approaching figure, now radiating an aura of immense power and quiet stoicism. Surya Dev, his face etched with a hint of nervousness, rose from his throne to greet his son.

Shani descended from the chariot, his dark eyes sweeping across the assembled celestial beings. A tremor of unease ran through the court as his gaze lingered on each being, a silent reminder of their karmic debts. Some fidgeted nervously, their expressions betraying past transgressions. Others met his gaze with unwavering righteousness, their hearts clear and their conscience untroubled.

Chhaya Rani, her eyes glistening with unshed tears, rushed forward and embraced her son. Shani, for a fleeting moment, allowed himself to feel the warmth of her love, a comforting reminder of the compassion that resided within him.

Surya Dev stepped forward, his voice tinged with a hint of formality. "Shani," he boomed, "you have come a long way. We are all here to witness the beginning of your celestial duty."

Shani bowed his head in respect. "Esteemed Father," he replied, his voice a low rumble, "I am but a humble servant of the cosmic order."

A murmur of surprise rippled through the court. The once-isolated child, who had inspired fear and unease, now spoke with humility and a profound sense of purpose. The weight of his destiny had not corrupted him; it had imbued him with wisdom and a deep understanding of his role in the cosmos.

Surya Dev, a flicker of pride in his eyes, addressed the celestial court. "From this day forward," he declared, "Shani Dev, the embodiment of karma, shall oversee the balance of justice. His gaze shall be a reminder of our actions and their consequences. Let us all respect his judgment and strive to live righteously."

A wave of acceptance washed over the celestial court. Shani Dev, the once-feared child, was now a respected figure, a vital cog in the machinery of the cosmos. His journey from an anomaly to the upholder of justice was complete. Yet, his true test was about to begin. The vast expanse of the cosmos awaited, filled with beings whose actions needed to be weighed on the scales of karma.

Shani Dev, with a resolute heart and a compassionate gaze, was prepared to face the challenges that lay ahead.

Chapter 3: The Scales of Karma

Shani Dev, the embodiment of karma, ascended his celestial chariot, the obsidian crows cawing a haunting melody as they propelled him towards the celestial expanse. His heart resonated with a quiet determination. He had undergone rigorous training, mastered his power, and received the blessings of Brahma Dev. Now, it was time to embark on his celestial duty – to ensure the cosmic scales remained balanced and that justice, however harsh, prevailed.

The vastness of the cosmos stretched before him, a shimmering tapestry of stars and celestial bodies. Shani Dev, his gaze ever-observant, scanned the various realms, his senses attuned to the karmic imbalances that rippled through the celestial fabric.

His first stop was Indra Loka, the resplendent abode of Indra Dev, the king of the Devas. Indra Dev, a powerful warrior known for his valor, also possessed a streak of arrogance and a thirst for power. These flaws, though seemingly insignificant, had begun to tip the scales of karma ever so slightly.

Shani Dev descended upon Indra Loka, his arrival causing a stir amongst the celestial beings. Indra Dev, ever prideful, emerged from his opulent palace, his brow furrowed in a display of dominance.

"Shani Dev," boomed Indra Dev, his voice laced with a hint of condescension, "to what do we owe this unexpected visit?"

Shani Dev met Indra Dev's gaze with unwavering calmness. His dark eyes, devoid of judgment, held a profound wisdom. "Indra Dev," he replied, his voice a low rumble, "I come as a reminder. Your actions, however grand, have consequences. A slight imbalance in the scales of karma has been detected."

Indra Dev scoffed. "I, the king of the Devas, protector of the cosmos? Imbalanced scales? This is a ridiculous notion!"

Shani Dev remained unfazed by Indra Dev's outburst. "Your victories, Indra Dev," he explained, "have fueled a sense of arrogance. Your thirst for power has caused suffering amongst some celestial beings."

Indra Dev's expression hardened. He was not accustomed to being questioned, especially by a being he perceived as inferior. Yet, there was an undeniable power in Shani Dev's gaze, a truth that resonated deep within him.

"What do you propose I do?" Indra Dev finally asked, a hint of grudging respect creeping into his voice.

Shani Dev did not offer solutions or pronounce punishments. "The path to restoring balance lies within yourself, Indra Dev," he replied. "Introspection and a willingness to rectify past transgressions are the first steps."

With a final, knowing glance, Shani Dev turned and ascended his chariot. The crows cawed once more, and he vanished into the celestial expanse, leaving Indra Dev grappling with the weight of Shani Dev's words.

News of Shani Dev's visit to Indra Loka spread like wildfire through the celestial realm. The revelation that even the mighty Indra Dev, the king of Devas, was not immune to karmic imbalance sparked a wave of introspection.

Many celestial beings, previously blinded by their own power or privilege, began to examine their actions with a newfound awareness. Some, with a sense of shame, acknowledged past wrongdoings and initiated efforts to rectify them. Others, however, remained defiant, viewing Shani Dev's intervention as an encroachment on their celestial authority.

Among the latter was Surya Dev, Shani Dev's own father. Despite his initial acceptance of Shani Dev's role, a deep-seated unease gnawed at him. He couldn't shake the feeling that his son's power, while necessary, was a source of potential discord within the celestial realm.

Surya Dev, ever the embodiment of radiant warmth and unwavering justice, felt threatened by the prospect of his son wielding such a powerful tool of introspection. He saw it as a challenge to his own authority, a force that could potentially expose the flaws and shortcomings of even the most revered celestial beings.

This unease manifested in subtle ways. Surya Dev became more distant towards Shani Dev, their celestial interactions reduced to formalities. He found excuses to avoid discussions concerning Shani Dev's duties or the impact his gaze was having on the celestial court.

Chhaya Rani, ever the pillar of unwavering love and support, recognized her husband's disquiet. She understood his apprehension, the fear that Shani Dev's power could disrupt the established order. However, she also saw the necessity of their son's role. The scales of karma needed to be balanced, and no being, however powerful, was exempt from its scrutiny.

One evening, as Surya Dev sat brooding in his celestial chambers, Chhaya Rani approached him, her gentle presence a soothing balm. They sat in comfortable silence for a while, the only sound the crackling of celestial fire in the hearth.

Finally, Chhaya Rani spoke, her voice soft yet firm. "Surya Dev," she began, "I understand your worries about Shani Dev. His power is immense, and its impact on the celestial realm cannot be ignored."

Surya Dev sighed, his face etched with concern. "It is not just his power, Chhaya Rani," he confessed. "It is the discord it brings. The exposure of past transgressions, the questioning of established hierarchies – it disrupts the harmony of the celestial court."

Chhaya Rani placed a comforting hand on his arm. "Harmony, Surya Dev, is not the same as stagnation. True balance requires introspection and adaptation. Shani Dev's role, while seemingly disruptive, is ultimately necessary for the continued health of the cosmos."

Her words resonated with Surya Dev. He saw a glimmer of truth in her perspective. Perhaps, true acceptance of Shani Dev's role would require not just acknowledging its necessity, but also embracing the potential for growth it presented.

"You are right, Chhaya Rani," he conceded finally. "We must learn to adapt, to embrace the changes that Shani Dev's role may bring."

A flicker of warmth returned to Surya Dev's eyes. He may not have fully embraced Shani Dev's power, but he was willing to accept his role in the cosmic order. Chhaya Rani, her heart filled with relief, smiled warmly. They had taken a small but important step towards a more unified family, bound by the challenges and opportunities presented by Shani Dev's unique celestial calling.

As Shani Dev continued his celestial journey, the impact of his gaze rippled throughout the cosmos. Some beings, humbled by his presence, sought atonement for past transgressions. Others, however, fueled by arrogance and a thirst for power, began to resist his influence.

This resistance culminated in a celestial upheaval that threatened to disrupt the very fabric of the cosmos.

Among the most vocal protestors was Rahu, a powerful asura (demon) known for his ambition and deceit. Rahu, along with a band of rebellious asuras, challenged Shani Dev's authority, claiming his gaze was an instrument of tyranny rather than justice.

"Why should we be subjected to this humiliation?" Rahu boomed, his voice echoing through the celestial expanse. "We are powerful beings, capable of shaping our own destinies. This Shani Dev, with his judgmental gaze, seeks to control us!"

Rahu's words resonated with some within the celestial court, particularly those who harbored resentment towards Shani Dev's role. A murmur of dissent began to spread, a growing wave of discontent threatening to engulf the once-harmonious cosmos.

News of the rebellion reached Surya Loka, casting a shadow of worry upon the celestial abode. Chhaya Rani, her ever-present maternal concern heightened, expressed her fear for Shani Dev's safety.

"Surya Dev," she pleaded, "this rebellion could escalate. Shani Dev, alone, might not be able to contain it."

Surya Dev, despite his lingering apprehension towards Shani Dev's power, understood the gravity of the situation. The potential for chaos in the cosmos was too great to ignore.

"We must act," he declared, his voice resolute. "Shani Dev may embody karma, but upholding the cosmic order requires unity. We must stand by him, regardless of our personal reservations."

With newfound determination, Surya Dev summoned the celestial army, a magnificent force of warriors clad in radiant armor. Together, they prepared to defend the principles of karma and justice that Shani Dev represented.

Meanwhile, Shani Dev, his gaze unwavering, confronted Rahu and his band of asuras. He remained impassive in the face of their insults and threats, his presence a silent embodiment of celestial law.

"Your defiance," Shani Dev finally spoke, his voice a low rumble, "only amplifies the karmic imbalances you seek to deny. Let go of your arrogance, Rahu, and seek redemption before your actions tip the scales beyond repair."

Rahu, fueled by rage and a warped sense of pride, refused to yield. "Redemption? I require none!" he roared. "We, the asuras, will carve our own destiny, free from your judgmental gaze!"

Seeing no other option, Shani Dev raised his hand, the power of karma crackling at his fingertips. It was a gesture of immense power, a warning of the consequences of unchecked rebellion.

Just as Shani Dev prepared to unleash his power, a blinding light erupted from the celestial expanse. Brahma Dev, the creator, had arrived, his presence radiating immense wisdom and authority.

"Silence!" boomed Brahma Dev's voice, shaking the very foundations of the cosmos. Both Shani Dev and the asuras fell silent, cowed by the creator's presence.

Brahma Dev addressed the celestial court, his voice filled with a deep sadness. "The cosmos thrives on balance," he intoned. "Justice and injustice, light and shadow, they all play a vital role in the celestial dance. To reject Shani Dev's role is to reject the very foundation of our existence."

He turned to Rahu and the asuras, his gaze holding a flicker of empathy. "Your anger stems from past injustices," he acknowledged. "But seeking revenge only breeds more suffering.

True power lies in introspection and the pursuit of a righteous path."

Brahma Dev's words resonated within the celestial court. The asuras, their defiance waning, began to see the folly of their rebellion. The truth of his words hung heavy in the air, a reminder that the path to true growth lay in embracing the principles Shani Dev represented.

The celestial crisis, as quickly as it arose, began to dissipate. Rahu and the asuras, humbled by Brahma Dev's wisdom, offered a reluctant truce. The rebellion, though a stark reminder of the challenges inherent in Shani Dev's role, ultimately served to reaffirm the importance of maintaining the cosmic balance.

THE AFTERMATH OF THE celestial upheaval ushered in a period of introspection within the cosmos. Beings of all walks of celestial life, from the mighty Devas to the rebellious asuras, grappled with the implications of Shani Dev's role.

Shani Dev himself remained a stoic figure, his gaze a constant reminder of the karmic consequences of actions. Yet, beneath his impassive exterior, there simmered a newfound understanding. The rebellion had revealed the fragility of the cosmic balance and the deep-seated resentment that could fester when beings felt judged or ignored.

Surya Dev, his earlier apprehension replaced by a newfound respect, approached Shani Dev. "Son," he began, his voice tinged with a hint of humility, "the past few days have shed light on the complexities of your role. You face not just resistance to justice, but also the burden of those who seek atonement."

Shani Dev inclined his head in acknowledgement. "Indeed, Father," he replied, his voice a low rumble. "The path of karma is not paved with judgment alone. It is also about offering guidance to those who seek to rectify past wrongs."

A new resolve settled upon Shani Dev. He understood that his gaze, while a powerful tool for justice, could also be an instrument of redemption. By offering insight into their karmic imbalances, he could guide beings towards a path of self-correction and restore balance not just externally, but also within their own hearts.

This newfound understanding manifested in subtle ways. When confronted with beings burdened by guilt, Shani Dev's gaze softened, offering a glimpse of the path to atonement. He began to offer cryptic prophecies, not as pronouncements of doom, but as warnings and opportunities for course correction.

The celestial court, initially wary of this shift, began to witness the positive impact. Beings who had previously resisted Shani Dev now sought his counsel, eager to understand the karmic consequences of their actions and the steps they could take towards redemption.

As news of Shani Dev's evolving role spread, a sense of cautious optimism filled the cosmos. The rebellion had served as a catalyst for change, fostering a deeper understanding of karma and the role it played in maintaining cosmic harmony.

However, the path to complete acceptance was long and arduous. There would always be those who chafed under Shani Dev's gaze, those who sought to shirk responsibility for their actions. Yet, with each passing day, Shani Dev's presence became less of a harbinger of misfortune and more of a symbol of karmic balance, a reminder that true justice, in all its complexity, was essential for the well-being of the cosmos.

The story of Shani Dev continues, his journey far from over. The vast expanse of the cosmos holds countless beings, each with their own karmic burdens. As Shani Dev navigates this complex celestial landscape, he will continue to evolve, his role in upholding the cosmic order forever etched in the celestial tapestry.

Chapter 4: Echoes of Mortality

Eons flowed by, measured not by the rise and fall of celestial bodies, but by the ebb and flow of karmic debts. Shani Dev, the embodiment of karma, had become an integral part of the cosmic order. His gaze, once feared, was now understood as a necessary force for balance, a reminder of the consequences attached to every action.

However, Shani Dev's celestial existence remained detached from the mortal realm, a world shrouded in mists of ignorance and fleeting pleasures. Little did he know, his presence and influence would soon be felt beyond the celestial expanse, echoing in the lives of a young human king named Vikramaditya.

Vikramaditya, a king renowned for his wisdom and righteousness, ruled his kingdom with a benevolent hand. His subjects thrived under his just reign, and peace reigned throughout the land. Yet, a nagging doubt gnawed at Vikramaditya's heart. He yearned for a deeper understanding of life, death, and the intricate workings of karma.

One starlit night, as Vikramaditya sat pondering the mysteries of existence, a celestial messenger materialized before him. The messenger, adorned in shimmering robes and radiating an otherworldly glow, bowed low before the king.

"Esteemed Vikramaditya," the messenger boomed, his voice echoing in the stillness of the night, "greetings from the celestial court. Your righteous rule and unwavering pursuit of justice have caught the attention of Shani Dev himself."

Vikramaditya, his heart pounding with a mixture of awe and trepidation, rose from his throne. "A message from Shani Dev?" he stammered. "What honor is this?"

The messenger smiled, his celestial features radiating warmth. "Shani Dev," he explained, "has observed your unwavering dedication to justice. He believes you hold the potential to bridge the gap between the celestial and mortal realms, to become a vessel for karmic understanding."

Vikramaditya's brow furrowed in contemplation. "A bridge?" he echoed, his voice filled with curiosity. "How can a mere mortal play such a role?"

The messenger chuckled softly. "Though you are mortal, Vikramaditya," he said, "your wisdom and righteousness transcend the limitations of your form. Shani Dev offers you a choice: embark on a celestial journey, witness the workings of karma firsthand, and return to your kingdom with a newfound understanding of the universe."

The enormity of the offer settled upon Vikramaditya. A celestial journey, a glimpse into the workings of karma – it was an opportunity beyond compare. Yet, the thought of leaving his kingdom and his people filled him with apprehension.

VIKRAMADITYA WRESTLED with the celestial messenger's offer. The promise of witnessing the workings of karma was an irresistible lure for a king who yearned for a deeper understanding of the world. Yet, the responsibility of his kingdom weighed heavily on him. Could he abandon his people for a celestial quest, however noble?

He looked around his chambers, the familiar sight offering a strange comfort. The maps adorning the walls, charting the vastness of his kingdom, reminded him of the lives he had sworn to protect. The scent of incense, used during his nightly meditations, grounded him in the familiar rhythm of his mortal existence.

"How long would this celestial journey take?" Vikramaditya finally asked, his voice betraying a hint of the conflict raging within him.

The celestial messenger, his expression patient, replied, "Time is measured differently in the celestial realm, Your Majesty. Your journey could last a day or a thousand years, but upon your return, you will find your kingdom untouched by the passage of mortal time."

Vikramaditya's eyes widened. The prospect of returning to a kingdom unchanged, a testament to the kingly council he had left behind, was enticing. But the thought of a thousand years passing in the blink of an eye made him pause. What would become of his legacy? Would his people remember him, or would he fade into a distant memory?

The messenger seemed to sense his concern. "Your legacy, Your Majesty, will not be forgotten. Your just rule has sown the seeds of a prosperous future for your kingdom. Your journey will only further your understanding and equip you to lead your people with even greater wisdom."

Vikramaditya's gaze fell upon a portrait of his young daughter, her innocent eyes filled with a child's trust. The future of the kingdom rested not just on his shoulders, but on hers as well. Perhaps, this celestial journey could provide him with the knowledge and tools to prepare her for the challenges that lay ahead.

With a deep breath, Vikramaditya straightened his posture, a newfound resolve settling within him. "I accept," he declared, his voice firm. "Tell Shani Dev that Vikramaditya, King of Justice, is ready to embark on this celestial journey."

A smile spread across the celestial messenger's face. "A wise decision, Your Majesty," he boomed. "Prepare yourself, for your journey begins at dawn."

As the celestial messenger dissolved into a swirl of stars, leaving Vikramaditya alone in his chambers, a wave of excitement mixed with trepidation washed over the king. He knew his life was about to change irrevocably. He was about to step into the unknown, a mortal king venturing into the celestial realm to unravel the mysteries of karma.

As dawn painted the horizon with streaks of gold and rose, Vikramaditya stood ready in the royal courtyard. He had donned his finest attire, a regal garment woven with threads of gold and shimmering with the blessings of his kingdom's wise men. Yet, beneath the regal facade, a tremor of nervousness ran through him.

Suddenly, a blinding light erupted in the center of the courtyard. As the light subsided, a celestial chariot materialized, its form crafted from stardust and drawn by four majestic swans with wings that shimmered like pearlescent clouds. A figure cloaked in obsidian robes stood beside the chariot, his posture radiating an air of quiet dignity.

"Vikramaditya, King of Justice," the figure boomed, his voice a low rumble that resonated with an otherworldly power. "I am Ketu, one of the Navagrahas, the nine celestial bodies that govern fate. I will be your guide on this journey."

Vikramaditya bowed his head in respect. The Navagrahas, of which Shani Dev was one, were revered figures in the celestial realm, their influence shaping the destinies of both mortals and immortals. To have one as his guide was an immense honor.

As Vikramaditya climbed into the chariot, a wave of dizziness washed over him. The celestial vehicle soared into the sky, leaving behind the familiar landscape of his kingdom and propelling him towards the unknown expanse of the cosmos.

Ketu, his face obscured by the hood of his cloak, remained silent throughout the journey. Vikramaditya, despite his initial apprehension, found himself strangely comforted by his stoic presence. It was a silence that spoke volumes, a promise of a journey filled not just with wonder, but also with the harsh realities of karma.

Their journey took them past celestial bodies of unimaginable beauty – swirling nebulae, star clusters that resembled celestial gardens, and planets bathed in an ethereal glow. Each sight filled Vikramaditya with awe, a testament to the vastness and complexity of the universe.

But amidst the beauty, Vikramaditya also witnessed the consequences of unchecked desires and unrepentant actions. He saw celestial beings frozen in time, their forms a stark reminder of past transgressions. He witnessed fiery infernos, the aftereffects of celestial wars fueled by greed and power.

Ketu, though silent, offered no explanations. He simply allowed Vikramaditya to witness the tapestry of karma unfold before him, its threads woven with both joy and suffering, light and darkness.

As days bled into eons, a profound transformation began to take root within Vikramaditya. The once-sheltered king was evolving into a being with a deeper understanding of the universe and the intricate dance of karma. He saw the consequences of his own actions, both just and unjust, reflected back at him in the celestial tapestry.

Finally, after a period that seemed to encompass both a lifetime and a fleeting moment, the celestial chariot began its descent. Below them, a magnificent city shimmered with an ethereal light – Surya Loka, the abode of the Sun god and the gateway to the heart of the celestial realm.

The celestial chariot glided gracefully through the pearly gates of Surya Loka, coming to rest in a courtyard paved with shimmering moonstone. Vikramaditya, his senses overwhelmed by the sheer vibrancy of the celestial city, disembarked, his mortal form feeling strangely heavy against the weight of his newfound knowledge.

Ketu, his obsidian cloak swirling around him, led Vikramaditya through a labyrinthine network of celestial gardens, each one bursting with exotic flora that shimmered with otherworldly radiance. Finally, they reached a magnificent palace, its walls adorned with tapestries depicting the cosmic dance of creation and destruction.

"We are here," Ketu said, his voice a low rumble. "Prepare yourself, King Vikramaditya. You are about to meet Shani Dev, the embodiment of karma."

A tremor of anxiety ran through Vikramaditya. He had witnessed the consequences of karma firsthand, but to stand before its very embodiment filled him with a sense of awe and trepidation.

Ketu ushered him into a grand hall, its ceiling adorned with constellations that shimmered like scattered diamonds. A throne of polished obsidian sat at the far end, seemingly carved from the very essence of night. Seated upon it was Shani Dev, his dark form radiating an aura of immense power.

Vikramaditya bowed low, his voice filled with respect as he addressed the celestial being. "Esteemed Shani Dev," he began, "King Vikramaditya, humbled by your invitation, stands before you."

Shani Dev inclined his head slightly, his gaze, usually a source of unease, holding a hint of curiosity. "Vikramaditya, King of Justice," he rumbled, his voice echoing in the vast hall. "Your journey through the celestial realm has been a testament to your unwavering spirit."

Vikramaditya straightened, a newfound confidence blossoming within him. "The journey has been an eye-opener, Shani Dev," he declared. "I have witnessed the vastness of the cosmos and the intricate workings of karma."

Shani Dev's gaze softened slightly. "Tell me, Vikramaditya," he asked, "what have you learned from your celestial sojourn?"

Vikramaditya recounted his experiences – the awe-inspiring beauty of the celestial realm, the harsh realities of karmic consequences, and the profound understanding of the interconnectedness of all things.

As he spoke, Shani Dev listened intently, his expression unreadable. When Vikramaditya finished, a moment of profound silence settled upon the hall.

Finally, Shani Dev spoke, his voice imbued with the wisdom of eons. "You have learned well, King Vikramaditya. Karma is not just about punishment, but also about growth and redemption. It is a force that guides us towards a balanced existence."

He extended a hand, his touch cool and ethereal. "Return to your mortal realm, King Vikramaditya. Take the knowledge you have gained and use it to not just govern your kingdom justly, but also to illuminate the path of karma for your people."

Vikramaditya bowed once more, his heart filled with gratitude. "Thank you, Shani Dev," he rasped, "for this invaluable gift of knowledge."

With a final nod, Shani Dev dismissed him. Ketu reappeared, and together they journeyed back to the celestial chariot. The descent back to Vikramaditya's kingdom was swift, a testament to the timelessness of the celestial realm.

As the chariot touched down upon familiar soil, Vikramaditya stepped out, no longer just a king, but a vessel of karmic understanding. He looked upon his kingdom with fresh eyes, ready to lead his people not just with justice, but also with the wisdom gleaned from his celestial odyssey. The journey had changed him irrevocably, and his reign, forever marked by his encounter with Shani Dev, would usher in a new era of enlightenment for his kingdom.

Chapter 5: The Ripple Effect

Vikramaditya, King of Justice, returned to his mortal realm a changed man. The celestial journey, orchestrated by Shani Dev himself, had imbued him with a profound understanding of karma and its intricate workings. He no longer saw justice as a mere act of punishment, but as a force for restoration and balance.

His kingdom, upon his return, remained untouched by the passage of time. The council he had appointed had ruled with wisdom and foresight, ensuring stability and prosperity. Yet, a subtle shift had occurred. The whispers of Vikramaditya's celestial journey had reached every corner of the kingdom, sparking curiosity and a yearning for a deeper understanding of the universal laws.

Vikramaditya, recognizing this yearning, embarked on a series of royal tours. He visited bustling marketplaces and serene temples, grand palaces and humble villages. Wherever he went, he spoke not just of earthly laws and governance, but also of the celestial laws of karma.

He explained how every action, good or bad, had a consequence, not just in the present but also rippling through the fabric of existence. He spoke of the importance of right conduct, of compassion and forgiveness, for true justice lay not just in punishment, but also in the opportunity for redemption.

His words, imbued with the wisdom gleaned from his celestial odyssey, resonated with his people. Farmers, artisans, and scholars alike found themselves contemplating the karmic implications of their actions. A wave of introspection washed over the kingdom, prompting a reevaluation of choices and a renewed commitment to ethical living.

Vikramaditya didn't stop at mere pronouncements. He established royal courts dedicated not just to legal disputes, but also to karmic imbalances. Wise men and women, trained in the principles of karma, offered guidance and facilitated reconciliation between those harboring grudges or seeking atonement for past transgressions.

These karmic courts, though initially met with skepticism, soon became a cornerstone of Vikramaditya's reign. People found solace in the opportunity to confess their wrongdoings and seek forgiveness. The kingdom, once governed solely by earthly laws, began to embrace a more holistic approach to justice, one that acknowledged the interconnectedness of actions and their consequences.

News of Vikramaditya's reign, marked by an infusion of celestial wisdom and a focus on karmic balance, spread beyond the borders of his kingdom. Neighboring rulers, intrigued by this novel approach to justice, sent emissaries to learn from his example.

Slowly, a ripple effect began to spread across the mortal realm. Kingdoms, once locked in petty squabbles and fueled by vengeance, started considering the karmic consequences of their actions. Disputes were settled through dialogue and mediation, with an emphasis on restoring balance rather than inflicting punishment.

Years turned into decades, and Vikramaditya's reign became a beacon of karmic justice. His kingdom, once a model of earthly law, transformed into a society built upon ethical principles and the pursuit of karmic equilibrium. Merchants avoided deceptive practices, warriors fought with honor, and disputes were resolved amicably, with both parties striving for understanding and reconciliation.

However, the path of karmic balance wasn't without its challenges. There were those who scoffed at the concept of karma, dismissing it as mere superstition. Some powerful nobles, accustomed to wielding authority through fear and intimidation, chafed under the constraints of karmic courts.

Vikramaditya, though a just ruler, remained a mortal king. He faced rebellions and internal conflicts fueled by greed and ambition. Yet, in these moments of turbulence, the lessons learned on his celestial journey proved invaluable.

He employed diplomacy whenever possible, reminding his adversaries that true victory lay not in dominating others, but in restoring balance and fostering peace. He used the threat of karmic consequences to deter aggression and encouraged his people to see conflict as an opportunity for growth and karmic cleansing.

Vikramaditya's reign wasn't devoid of punishments. But when necessary, they were administered not with vengeance but with a view to restoring balance. Criminals were given the opportunity to atone for their deeds through community service or acts of charity. This approach, while initially met with resistance, eventually fostered a sense of responsibility and a stronger sense of community within the kingdom.

As Vikramaditya aged, his hair turned white and his steps grew slower. Yet, his spirit remained strong, his commitment to karmic justice unwavering. He continued to guide his people, his wisdom a beacon of hope in times of hardship.

One evening, as Vikramaditya sat in his royal gardens, gazing at the celestial expanse, a familiar figure materialized before him. It was Ketu, the Navagraha who had guided him on his celestial journey.

"King Vikramaditya," Ketu boomed, his voice echoing in the stillness of the evening. "Your reign has been a testament to the power of karmic understanding. You have not only ruled your kingdom justly but also inspired others to embrace the principles of balance and right conduct."

A warm smile graced Vikramaditya's aging face. "It has been a journey filled with challenges, Ketu," he rasped, his voice weakened by age. "But the rewards have been immense. My people have embraced a way of life that transcends mere earthly laws."

Ketu nodded his hooded head. "The seeds of karma you have sown will continue to blossom long after your reign ends. Your legacy, King Vikramaditya, will be one of justice, compassion, and a commitment to understanding the interconnectedness of all things."

As Vikramaditya looked up at the star-dusted night sky, a sense of peace washed over him. He knew his time as king was nearing its end, but the impact of his reign would echo through generations to come. His encounter with Shani Dev and the celestial journey that followed had not only changed him but also shaped the destiny of his entire kingdom. And as he closed his eyes for the last time, Vikramaditya, the King of Justice, knew his legacy would live on in the hearts of his people, forever guided by the principles of karma.

Centuries flowed by after Vikramaditya's reign. Kingdoms rose and fell, empires crumbled and reformed, yet the echoes of karmic justice lingered in the mortal realm. His approach to governance, documented in detailed scrolls and passed down through generations, became a source of inspiration for rulers across the land.

One such ruler, Queen Amara, a woman known for her wisdom and compassion, ascended the throne of a neighboring kingdom. Inheriting a land rife with corruption and internal strife, Queen Amara sought guidance in the ancient texts chronicling Vikramaditya's reign.

The scrolls spoke of a king who ruled not just with earthly laws but also with an understanding of karma. They detailed the karmic courts he established, where individuals sought reconciliation and atonement for past transgressions. Inspired by this approach, Queen Amara decided to implement a similar system.

She established a grand hall known as "The Hall of Karmic Balance," where wise judges, trained in Vikramaditya's principles, presided over disputes. These judges focused not just on finding fault, but on understanding the underlying causes of conflict and facilitating dialogue between the parties involved.

The concept of karmic consequences resonated with Queen Amara's people. They began to see their actions not just in the context of earthly laws, but also as ripples within the vast tapestry of existence. This newfound awareness fostered a sense of responsibility and a willingness to seek forgiveness and reconciliation.

However, the path to karmic balance was not without its challenges. Powerful nobles, accustomed to wielding absolute power, resisted the constraints of the karmic courts. They saw them as an infringement on their authority and a threat to their ill-gotten gains.

Queen Amara, though a wise ruler, faced numerous threats to her authority. Yet, she remained steadfast in her commitment to karmic justice. She used diplomacy and the power of persuasion, reminding her adversaries that true power lay not in domination but in fostering harmony and balance.

News of Queen Amara's reign, echoing Vikramaditya's legacy of karmic justice, spread far and wide. Other kingdoms, witnessing the prosperity and peace thriving within her borders, began to reevaluate their own approaches to governance. Slowly, the principles of karma, once dismissed as mere superstition, started gaining acceptance across the mortal realm.

Meanwhile, in the celestial realm, Shani Dev watched with a hint of satisfaction. Vikramaditya's journey and its ripple effect were not confined to a single kingdom. The seeds of karmic understanding, sown on mortal soil, were slowly taking root, shaping the destinies of countless lives.

The embodiment of karma, however, remained impassive. His gaze continued its relentless vigil, ensuring that the scales of balance never tipped too far in one direction. But within his impassive exterior, a flicker of hope resided. Perhaps, the day would come when the mortal realm, guided by the principles of karma, wouldn't require his constant observation. Perhaps, one day, true balance would be achieved.

The story of Vikramaditya and Queen Amara serves as a reminder that the impact of a single encounter, guided by wisdom and compassion, can reverberate for generations to come. It also highlights the transformative power of karma – a force that not only dictates consequences but also offers opportunities for growth and redemption, both for individuals and for entire societies. The echoes of Vikramaditya's reign, a testament to the interconnectedness of all things, continue to resonate within the vast tapestry of existence, a beacon of hope for a future where karma guides us all towards a more balanced and just world.

Centuries after Queen Amara's reign, the mortal realm remained a complex dance of light and shadow. While the principles of karma had taken root in many lands, pockets of corruption and injustice persisted. It was during this period of precarious balance that an unusual celestial phenomenon occurred.

Across the night sky, a startling alignment of planets took place. Shani Dev, the embodiment of karma, occupied a central position, his gaze radiating with an intensity unseen in eons. Astrologers across the mortal realm trembled, sensing the impending significance of this celestial convergence.

On a solitary mountaintop, a young woman named Maya meditated beneath the shimmering expanse. Unlike others who feared the celestial alignment, Maya felt a strange pull, a sense of destiny beckoning her. Unknown to her, she was a descendant of Queen Amara, a lineage steeped in the wisdom of karmic understanding.

As the planets reached their peak alignment, a blinding light erupted from the night sky. Maya, bathed in the celestial glow, felt a presence unlike anything she had ever encountered. When the light subsided, she found herself standing before Shani Dev, his imposing form casting a long shadow across the mountain peak.

"Maya," his voice boomed, echoing across the vastness of space, "descendant of Queen Amara, you have been chosen."

Maya, overwhelmed yet strangely unafraid, bowed her head. "Shani Dev," she stammered, "why have you chosen me?"

Shani Dev's gaze, usually a source of unease, softened slightly. "The mortal realm teeters on a precipice," he explained. "The balance of karma is threatened by those who wield power without understanding its consequences."

He gestured towards the shimmering expanse above. "The celestial alignment signifies a time of reckoning. A time for a mortal vessel to carry the message of karma back to their world."

A wave of realization washed over Maya. This wasn't a coincidence – it was a call to action. "What must I do?" she asked, her voice firm with newfound resolve.

Shani Dev imparted his knowledge – the intricacies of karma, the path to atonement, and the importance of fostering balance within the mortal realm. He imbued her with a portion of his celestial wisdom, a spark to ignite the fires of karmic understanding within the hearts of men.

As dawn painted the horizon with streaks of gold and rose, Maya found herself back on the mountaintop. The celestial alignment had passed, but within her, a new journey had begun.

Armed with the celestial knowledge bestowed upon her by Shani Dev, Maya descended from the mountaintop, no longer a solitary seeker but a vessel of karmic wisdom. She embarked on a quest, not to conquer kingdoms or amass wealth, but to spread the message of karma, to remind mortals of the interconnectedness of all things and the consequences of their actions.

Her journey would be arduous, fraught with challenges and opposition from those who benefited from the imbalance. Yet,

Maya, like Vikramaditya and Queen Amara before her, carried the torch of karmic justice.

And as she journeyed across the land, her message resonated with those yearning for a more balanced world. The echoes of Vikramaditya's reign, the seeds sown by Queen Amara, and the celestial touch of Shani Dev – all converged within Maya, a testament to the enduring power of karma and the potential for positive change within the ever-evolving saga of the mortal realm.

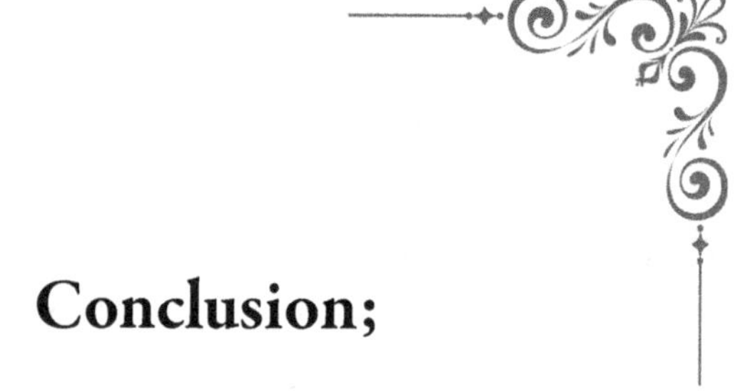

Conclusion;

As the final chapter closes, a profound understanding of karma's enduring power settles upon us. This journey has brought us face-to-face with the inescapable consequences of human actions, the ripples of good and ill deeds echoing through time.

The unwavering gaze of Shani Dev serves as a constant reminder – the universe maintains a delicate balance. Every decision, every act, carries weight, shaping the fabric of existence. Yet, within this framework lies the potential for redemption. Through self-awareness, atonement, and a commitment to righteous living, individuals can transform the karmic burdens they carry.

The story's echoes resonate beyond the narrative's boundaries. They serve as a call to action for us, the readers, to examine our own lives with honesty. Are we living in accordance with our highest values? Are we striving to make a positive impact on the world?

"In The Shadow of Shani Dev Ji" transcends the boundaries of a simple tale. It becomes a mirror reflecting the human condition, compelling us to confront our flaws, embrace our strengths, and ultimately, strive for a life aligned with the universal principles of karma.

The story may end, but the journey of self-discovery continues. May the lessons learned within these pages guide us towards a more balanced, just, and ultimately, enlightened existence. For even in the face of darkness, the potential for karmic transformation and a brighter future always lies within our grasp.

About the Author

Mrigendra Bharti, born on June 29, 2004, in South Delhi, India, is a multifaceted individual recognized as the owner of Mrigendra Bharti Group InfoTech India Co. Pvt Ltd. Beyond his entrepreneurial endeavors, he is a distinguished music producer, director, and a budding writer.

Embarking on his professional journey at a young age, Mrigendra Bharti's visionary leadership has led to the establishment of several successful ventures, including Croma Music Series Entertainment, Sellbrochure, Fauget Innovative, and more.

What sets Mrigendra apart is his early initiation into the world of business. His foray into the unknown realms of entrepreneurship began during his 10th-grade years, where he delved into the music industry. This initial venture laid the foundation for subsequent achievements, showcasing his dedication and resilience.

Having honed his skills in music, Mrigendra Bharti not only demonstrated significant growth in his craft but also expanded his professional network. His passion extends beyond music, encompassing app and website development, as well as graphic design.

Fueled by his creative aspirations, Mrigendra established the Mrigendra Bharti Group, a company specializing in website and app development. Currently, he collaborates with a dedicated team, collectively working on ambitious projects that promise innovation and excellence.

Mrigendra's journey serves as an inspiration, particularly for today's students, highlighting the potential of youthful determination and the ability to transform innovative ideas into successful businesses. As he continues to make strides in various domains, Mrigendra Bharti remains a dynamic force, contributing vibrancy to the realms of business, music, and technology.

Read more at https://www.imwriter-mrigendra.rf.gd.